This book belongs to:

_____

This book is based on the TV episode "The Most Perfect Parent," written by Steven Sullivan,
from the animated TV series *Miss Spider's Sunny Patch Friends* on Nick Jr.,
a Nelvana Limited/Absolute Pictures Limited co-production in association
with Callaway Arts & Entertainment, based on the Miss Spider books by David Kirk.

Nicholas Callaway, President and Publisher
Cathy Ferrara, Managing Editor and Production Director
Toshiya Masuda, Art Director • Nelson Gómez, Director of Digital Technology
Joya Rajadhyaksha, Editor • Amy Cloud, Editor
Bill Burg, Digital Artist • Christina Pagano, Digital Artist
Raphael Shea, Senior Designer • Krupa Jhaveri, Designer

Special thanks to the Nelvana staff, including Doug Murphy, Scott Dyer, Tracy Ewing, Pam Lehn,
Tonya Lindo, Mark Picard, Jane Sobol, Luis Lopez, Eric Pentz, and John Cvevich.

Library of Congress Cataloging-in-Publication Data available upon request.

Distributed in the United States by Penguin Young Readers Group.

Visit Callaway Arts & Entertainment at www.callaway.com

ISBN 978-0-448-44692-9

10 9 8 7 6 5 4 3 2 1   07 08 09 10

First edition, September 2007

Printed in China

The Most Perfect Parent

David Kirk

CALLAWAY

NEW YORK

2007

"Buggie baby buggy coming through!" Spindella said as she wheeled their three little spiderlings up the lane. "Don't forget that you have to watch the children while I'm away this weekend."

Spiderus assured his wife he'd be able to babysit *and* paint the lair.

Thwack! A berry ball hit the back of Spiderus's head. Paint spilled, and Bella giggled.

Then Mandrake asked him about flowers, and Ivy blew bubbles for him to admire. Spiderus didn't know which way to turn.

Shimmer and Squirt came by to see if they could help.

"I have everything under control," Spiderus told them, scooping up Bella and Ivy.

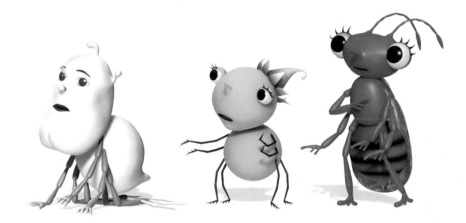

Squirt pointed out that Mandrake seemed to be left out, so Spiderus scurried over to his son.

"Da-dee, da-dee," Bella and Ivy called, reaching out for another hug.

Oh dear, Spiderus thought, am I ignoring the girls now? He began to wonder if twins needed special care.

"Ah, Miss Spider!" said Spiderus, seeing her in the meadow with Snowdrop and Pansy. He had a list of questions about the best way to raise twins.

Miss Spider assured him it was just like raising any other little bugs. "As long as you don't get their names mixed up," she added with a wink.

Nervous that he might confuse his twins, Spiderus attached a bell to Bella's head.

"This will help me remember which twin is which," Spiderus decided. "Bell, Bella."

"Ting-a-ling," cooed Mandrake.

"Ding-dong," Ivy chimed in.

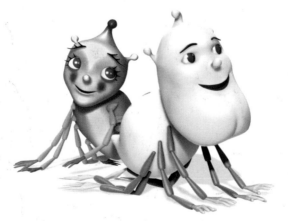

When Spiderus turned around to continue painting, Bella took off her bell and hung it on Ivy. The sisters giggled.

"Up to your tricks again, Bella?" Spiderus asked Ivy.

Giggling some more, she replied, "No Bella. Ivy."

Spiderus was totally confused!

Then Spiderus saw Holley and Squirt playing.

Squirt threw a ball too close to his father's head, and Holley told him to be more careful. Squirt said he was sorry.

Whipping out a notebook, Spiderus asked Holley, "How did you know how to discipline him?"

"Slow down," Holley chuckled.

He told Spiderus that all children are naughty sometimes. "Usually all that's needed to get them back to good buggie behavior is a firm word," he said. "That and the occasional time-out."

"Watch out!" Squirt cried.

Spiderus's little ones were misbehaving again. Mandrake was trying to push the buggy while his sisters jumped up and down.

"Oh dear," sighed Spiderus, "I guess I need to do some baby-bug proofing!"

After Spiderus had created a webby playpen, he tried to start painting again.

"Da-dee, drinkee," demanded Ivy.

"Papa, me hungry," cried Mandrake.

"Me sleepy!" sobbed Bella.

Soon all three babies were crying.

Even in the Cozy Hole, Miss Spider and Holley could hear the wails. Before they could offer to help, Spiderus was at their doorstep with three bawling buggies in his arms.

"Help!" he exclaimed.

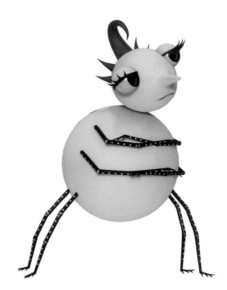

Suddenly, there was a loud crash from upstairs. The Spider children were playing holleyberry hockey instead of sleeping.

"Sounds like it might be time-out time," said Holley.

"So I'm not the only one who has trouble raising his little buggies?" Spiderus asked.

"Nobody's a perfect parent," Holley replied.

"As long as you love your spiderlings," Miss Spider added, "the rest will fall into place."

The next morning, Spindella returned home to splotches of paint all over the floor and walls!

"Any problems while I was away?" she asked.

"None at all," said Spiderus, smiling as the three spiderlings welcomed their mother home.

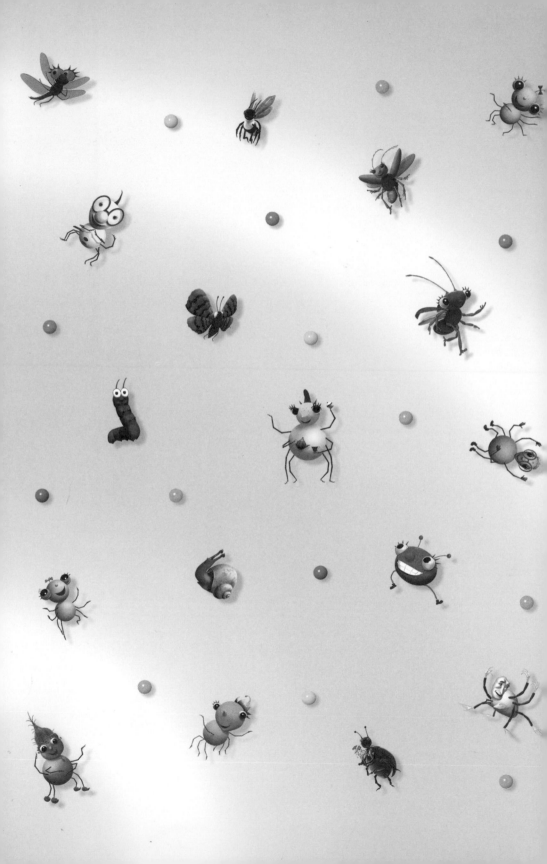